good deed rain

Books by Allen Frost

Ohio Trio
Bowl of Water
Another Life
Home Recordings
The Mermaid Translation
The Selected Correspondence of Kenneth Patchen
The Wonderful Stupid Man
Saint Lemonade
Playground
Roosevelt
5 Novels
The Sylvan Moore Show
Town in a Cloud
A Flutter of Birds Passing Through Heaven: A Tribute to Robert Sund
At the Edge of America
Lake Erie Submarine
The Book of Ticks
I Can Only Imagine
The Orphanage of Abandoned Teenagers
Different Planet
Go with the Flow: A Tribute to Clyde Sanborn
Homeless Sutra
The Lake Walker

THE LAKE WALKER

Allen Frost

The Lake Walker ©2018
Allen Frost, Good Deed Rain
Bellingham, Washington
ISBN 978-1-64204-538-3

Writing: Allen Frost
Cover & Photos of Lake Padden: Allen Frost
Technical Assistance: Fred Sodt
Cover Production: Katrina Svoboda Johnson
Apple: TFK!

THE LAKE WALKER

THE LAKE WALKER

The New Death
Rudolph & Simone
Social Services
The Wall
The Blue Balloon
Fishing
Wave
Questions
The Blind Man
Beverley
Deserts
Seeing Blue
The Meeting
Lynn
Minus One
The Mermaid
A Bird Book
Willard
Walking with a Wish

INTRODUCTION

Back in high school I would go to the Neptune Theatre every week. Driving the floating bridge over Lake Washington or going Lake City Way, looking for parking, sometimes under a leafy tree, sometimes on the slant by the IHOP. The Neptune had a green neon sign that floated out front. Inside, you bought your ticket from a boat shaped counter and then you could go up to the balcony. That's where I met Fellini, Bergman, Cocteau, and I wanted this adventure to be an homage to them, a sort of European black and white movie book.

This idea began during a hellish summer when forest fires turned our air into a white smog and the sun was dim as an orange penny. A Martian world, it was hard to even breathe out there. But by September it started to clear and I began to take walks around the lake. I still had a couple weeks away from my office job and I liked to think this would be my morning routine when I finally retire. I would begin every day with a walk around the lake.

-AF

His flower had told him that she was the only one of her kind in all the universe. And here were five thousand of them, all in one garden.

The Little Prince
Antoine de Saint-Exupéry

CHAPTER ONE:
The New Death

Death was dying. The old man sat heavy as a sack of iron on the bench.

Rudolph sat with him and they looked at the lake together.

The water was a mirror of the sky, crumpled like tinfoil where the breeze ruffled. Geese were out in the middle. A paddle boarder to the left crept along the edge of waterlily.

Rudolph listened to the sound of the lake. The old man breathed like a factory built next to it.

"Listen to me," the old man said. "You won't believe what I have to tell you." Death took another breath and his voice rattled as he exhaled. Talking wasn't easy for him. He would take a minute to make a sentence again.

Funny, the doctor told Rudolph walking would be good for his health and now here he was sitting with Death.

A path went all around Lake Pardon. It was 2.6 miles. Rudolph began every day making that circle. It was the end of a long summer and the weather was beautiful.

Leaving the tarred parking lot, Rudolph would start the circumnavigation. If you went east you would be in the sun for the first half—if you went west you would be in the forest for half an hour.

It was a mediation he looked forward to and every day had scenes like a movie along the way. Written on orange cones, a warning: Yellow Jackets Nest In Bank. Two crows going through the garbage left by the water, a sandwich bag in the line of foam on the shore. Like a train engineer, a baby in the front of a stroller. Another crow called from top an alder. Two women jogged past him. Two quiet stones on the edge of the lake, a good place to sit with someone. Through the leaves, a log in the water that the turtles liked. On the dock, too early for fishers, a heron stood on the bench at the end and turned his sharpened head to watch Rudolph. The footsteps and bits of conversation of those walking by. A little footbridge, the path a shallow creek. Fish departed beneath the reflection of green firs and cedars. Silver sky. Yellow leaves fallen off trees hanging over the water. It was cool on the treed side of the lake. Hammer of a woodpecker. Some people say hello to you, some don't—you never know. Kids on bikes thrilling to go fast. A panting, steam engine dog on a leash. A kingfisher laughing somewhere hidden. A garter snake resting on the path. A glimpse of the other side of the lake, the fence of cattails on the opposite shore. People talking about work, their voices fade. Ducks. At the west shore, the wind splashes little wave rills on the rocks. Sounds of water.

"My time here is over," the old man said. His arm moved towards Rudolph. "I choose you." His hand lay open on the bench. "You are the new Death."

Three ducks appeared in the shallows. Rudolph watched them instead. One of them bobbed under so all you could see was its tail and orange paddling feet.

The old man who introduced himself to Rudolph two days ago drew another slow breath.

In a way, Rudolph walked right into this. Death was always seated there when he passed and two days ago Rudolph stopped to rest. He said hello to the lonely looking old man at the other end of the bench. He thought he would be nice and talk about the weather. The path around the lake was stocked with characters. Who knew what the old man would have to say? He looked at Rudolph and right away said, "My name is Death."

After that, Rudolph avoided him for a while.

Behind the bench, a boy walked by dragging a stick, scratching dirt and gravel.

Rudolph guessed the old man who called himself Death wasn't going anywhere. His breath still wheezed and rasped. It would be okay to leave.

"Well, it was nice seeing you again," Rudolph said, "but I better be going." He didn't want to wait around for the next sentence to roll of the assembly line. He stood up and left the old man steaming. Death was dying but he wasn't dead yet.

CHAPTER 2:
Rudolph & Simone

You start to notice the same people—when you have a routine, you find out others do too. That's how Rudolph met Simone. Every morning after she dropped her older daughter off at school, she would come to the lake with her baby. Rudolph took notice of her stroller right away. Her baby was wrapped in a French flag blanket. "Bonjour!" Rudolph greeted them and Simone had a beautiful smile. They had both slowed without even knowing, as if invisible gears had begun to mesh and pull them together.

"Bonjour," she smiled back. "Do you speak French?"

"Oh no. I can only say hello. I can tell you know more." He meant her accent, the voice he would look forward to hearing every morning from then on. They became friends instantly. Every day they would meet along the path and walk together and talk.

Mostly he liked to listen to her story. She had been places he could only dream about now. She was born in Martinique and went to school in Paris. From all that sun and sea to those old stone lined streets is how he pictured it. He had to admit, seeing her was the best part of the lake.

Especially after listening to Death. Then he couldn't wait to see her again.

They never made an appointment to meet, but they would rendezvous somewhere along the path. There was only 3 miles of it, it wasn't infinite. Though if you thought about it, it was pretty amazing that all her globe travels would bring her to cross paths with him.

Rudolph was 65 and newly retired and had never left town in thirty years.

The path turned around some tall trees and he could see a long stretch of the gravel ahead. Some joggers were approaching. Someone was walking a black dog. No sign of Simone and her stroller. Where was she? Maybe he needed new glasses, he thought, ones specially made with radar that could find her. He would see a glow in the corner of his eye and know she was near.

A striped beach ball was left in the reeds near the water. It was waiting for someone too.

What if she started walking the same direction as him? She could be a couple hundred yards ahead of him and they wouldn't meet. He might see the dot of her across the long dry baseball field where the path ducked into the woods. That's why each day they would circle the lake the opposite way so they would be sure to connect. But she could have forgot. Or what if he did? He was supposed to go to the left today, wasn't he? What if Death threw him off? Got him turned around?

"Rudolph!"

She was coming down the hill from the parking lot. It was perfect timing after all.

He waited for her. The lady with the black dog passed him and said hello. It was mostly women at the lake at this hour.

"Hi Simone!" Rudolph waved.

Her daughter Sylvie saw it was him and she smiled; those eyes the same as her mother's. The stroller bumped but she held onto her blanket.

"I am sorry we are a little late today."

Rudolph said, "That's okay. I'm so glad to see you. I like your scarf," he added. It was sky blue, with stars, and it wrapped over her hair, tied below her chin. "I thought you might not show up."

She touched his arm and everything was okay. They started around the lake together. 2.6

miles started from there.

"I just left Death," Rudolph said. "He's back there."

"Let's hope he is gone by the time we get there."

Rudolph agreed.

"You know," she said, "I still have not met him."

"I know. Lucky you."

She laughed.

Some ducks landed in the shallow water close to shore. They wore white stripes and some other colors. It wasn't easy to know all the different birds. He had a book he got at the library, but he left it at home, his room at the Evergreen Motel. Like those birds, he was adrift from place to place. He didn't want roots anymore. Now that he was retired he wanted to be free. He sold the house he used to live in, and he waited to see what would happen next. Everything was simple. He walked around the lake for his health, to be with Simone. She made him happy and free like one of those birds.

When they got to the playground, Simone parked the stroller so Sylvie could watch the kids playing there. Her little hands would hold out to them and her legs would kick. A dog barked, waiting for its ball to be thrown. Everything was waiting for the next thing to happen.

Rudolph and Simone talked for a while. Every day he would go somewhere listening to her. When Sylvie kicked her blanket off onto the ground, Simone decided it was time to walk again. The path took them around the baseball field, behind the chain link wall at home plate. Two boys were playing with their mom. A hit sent her running and the boys were cheating to turn it into a homerun.

Someone passed by them briskly and Simone whispered, "Did you see that?"

"No." Rudolph turned.

"She had a dog in her purse."

All Rudolph could see was her back to them. "I didn't look at her." She was in such a sour-faced hurry, he had looked away. Some people don't want to say hello, he figured she was one of them.

"A little dog looking out," Simone laughed. "She looked like a kangaroo!"

"Oh great, I missed it." Rudolph turned again but the woman was small as an inch in the distance. "Maybe we'll see her again."

"I'm not so sure. I think she has somewhere to be."

"That's the way it is with kangaroos."

They entered the shadows on the edge of the forest. From here on, the path stayed in the trees, with the lake only seen through the leaves.

They had a favorite place where they would stop, a bench surrounded by all the emerald mossy firs and cedars. Like a couch in a green room, it was halfway along the south side of the lake and by the time they got there and stopped Sylvie was almost asleep. It wouldn't be long before Babar, or Madeline or some other book her mother brought along would carry her off. The sound of those words in French, the warm shade of the lake, all she had to do was close her eyes. Today though it wasn't elephants or girls lined up in rows. Simone held the book for Rudolph to see. It was a story he asked her to read, one he loved but he never heard in its original language.

"Le Petit Prince," she said and turned the page.

He looked at Sylvie. Her eyes were closed. He closed his too and listened.

"Sa fleur lui avait raconté qu'elle était seule de son espèce dans l'univers. Et voici qu'il en était cinq mille, toutes semblables, dans un seul jardin!"

CHAPTER THREE:
Social Services

Rudolph waved as their car left the parking lot. They were followed by the jingling electronic song of a van selling ice cream. The windows were covered in bright decals. A woman wearing a head scarf drove. It moved slowly, with a line of cars behind it. More people were showing up. There were even some swimmers now. Someone carried a yellow kayak past him.

Rudolph followed that banana-looking boat down the weedy hill to the familiar path. When he said goodbye to Simone and Sylvie, it meant the end of his day at the lake and time to go home too.

He backtracked, noticing the same sights again. The way to his motel was along the path a little more, then through the lot and across the road.

"Hi Rudolph," a girl said as she jogged by. That was Lynn. She worked part time at the desk at the Evergreen. He touched the brim of his fedora—the hat kept his eyes in the shade and also gave him the look of a 1940s private eye, an impression he didn't dispel with the rumpled charcoal suit he wore. Who dressed like that now?

The same guy was still fishing from a folding chair set on the sand. Rudolph had seen the herons stare at the water that way.

Simone was right—Death wasn't on his bench when they passed before, and he still wasn't.

Rudolph paused at the bench anyway. A cool breeze blew ripples across the lake towards him, knocking the cattail stalks, stirring the leaves like a witch's broom. Where had that old man gone?

He couldn't have gone far—unless he was stretchered away to a hospital. That seemed probable, but Rudolph took a few more steps to see if Death had crawled into the underbrush to die. Maybe there would be toadstools grown in the form of his collapse.

"Rudolph."

The hoary sound of his name made him jump.

Death leaned against the cracked trunk of an oak, not more than five feet away. He wasn't exactly terrifying in his sweater and checkered pants—he looked frail enough to be kited by the wind—but his voice seemed to carry from somewhere deep and dark and underground. "Do you remember what I told you?"

For over thirty years Rudolph sat behind a desk, listening to stories, being compassionate, filling out paperwork that would help sort out so many lives. He had an ear for misery, which is why he sat with the old man who called himself Death and heard him out. Most people would have avoided him, would have turned their attention to anything else instead.

"You said you chose me for something," Rudolph answered. His mouth had gone dry, his throat suddenly felt raw. It was the strangest sensation.

The old man's eyes blistered. "You will learn what you need to do. You will see a blue glow and you will know."

"Okay," Rudolph said. There was no cause for alarm. He held his hands opened and calm. He used to see people like Death every day and he got used to them. What was unexpected was what happened next.

The old man backed up against the tree—backed into the tree—he actually melted into the bark in two steps and was gone.

Rudolph's held out hands were numb. Buzzing with that dumb electricity, he stared at the shadows carved into the rough trunk. Thirty years working for social services and he had never seen that happen in his office.

Out on the lake, a pair of oars clacked against wood. Some rowing scull had stopped, to glide across a perfect mirror of sky.

flow into a tree

CHAPTER FOUR:
The Wall

Every leaf on the big oak tree had turned crisp and red. As he hurried away, Rudolph tried to convince himself that's the way they already were. A man couldn't just flow into a tree, and summer couldn't end with a snap. There were two girls sunbathing on the grass. There were kids with buckets on the sand.

The path was met with a stairway that Rudolph quickly took. It led him to the parking lot and he walked by the shining cars. He could hear the ball on the tennis court going back and forth, then a yell when it stopped. He stepped from the tar onto a dirt trail. He was trying not to think about Death. He looked at the ripe blackberries, and the bare huckleberry branches. Their fruit was gone, picked off by little birds. He heard a car rush past on the road ahead. He would have to cross and walk along the shoulder. The Evergreen Motel wasn't far. It had a large white sign with green letters. He could have seen it from the trail if not for all the leaves.

"You are the new Death." That's what the

old man told him. It was the sort of crazy thing that stayed with you, rode on your shoulder like a crow.

Rudolph pushed a branch aside and he stopped at the roadside.

A crow flew overhead, wingtips spread like black fingers.

Rudolph thought of his room...the carpeting, the bed, the window curtains and TV. He would make a sandwich and watch the 1 o'clock movie like he always did.

But something strange was happening. He could not step onto the street. It was safe—there was only one truck, far down to his right, and he had plenty of time to cross. So what's the matter with me? he asked. He backed up and tried again, but he was running into an invisible wall. He could push his hands along it. His fingers and palms buzzed numbly again.

A car approached from his left. He retreated to the dirt trail and let it roar past. The truck from the right also came and went. Rudolph could feel their wakes. What kind of a wall was it? Well...he thought, I can try to figure it out. Wasn't he dressed as a detective? Shouldn't he play the part?

For his first test, with a bit of a groan he

picked up a fir cone. He let another couple cars rush by and when the coast was clear, he tossed the cone at the wall. It wasn't a wall. The fir cone skittered out to the yellow painted line.

He tried a broken branch. He could hold it into the road just fine until his knuckles were stopped by something in the air.

"Is it only me?" he asked. There was no sidekick next to him to answer. Could it be just this spot that was giving him trouble?

Rudolph walked along in the gravel and occasionally he would reach towards the road. Again and again, his hand was stopped.

And he was making progress towards the Evergreen Motel. Pretty soon it was right across from him. Did he need a catapult to get there? Would he ever get to his room and his sandwich? Not that he was hungry…

"Hi Rudolph."

She surprised him again. It was Lynn, returning from her run around the lake. Her face was flush and her bare skin shined. "Ah youth," he almost said. Instead, he asked, "Are you going to the motel?"

"I start work in a half hour. Enough time for a shower. Are you going back?"

"Oh no. I don't think so, not yet."

"Okay," she smiled. "Well, I'll see you later then."

"I hope so."

She smiled at him again and checked the road before she ran across. It was effortless for her. She was only twenty though. She had years to catch up to him.

He did take a step forwards, hopefully.

The wall was still there.

He sighed. It was worth a try.

CHAPTER FIVE:
The Blue Balloon

Rudolph walked back towards the lake. What choice did he have? The wall would probably keep going, along the road, down the hill to the bay. If he got in a boat, would he find that it continued on the water too? Across to Lemon Island and onwards to Japan? And around the world?

He heard laughter in the trees. It wasn't exactly laughing, but that's what it sounded like. He stopped and searched the canopy and saw movement on the trunk of a Douglas fir. He didn't need his bird library book. It was a pileated woodpecker. It hopped up the bark in its long black coat, that red sharpened head darting about. Maybe it was laughing at him. He didn't blame it. Unlike people, a bird could go wherever it wanted. Rudolph had to admit, it was funny alright.

As he almost tripped on a root, Rudolph decided he better watch where he was going. The trail was sown with fir needles. He wondered how his bare feet would feel on them. Good, he bet. The saints of India would walk like that.

His foot nearly landed on a black beetle. It was overturned, on its back, and he wondered if it died that way. He gently pushed it with his shoe until it rolled over. "There you go," he said. Its legs moved feebly and the next thing you knew, it spun onto its back again. Rudolph gave it a tap and it failed again. It was like a broken toy. "Oh come on!" His shoe could help or send it to the next world. Then it turned blue. A foggy aura surrounded it. He didn't know much about bugs but it reminded him of a firefly. When he was a kid he remembered a field full of them at night.

He let himself drop down close, thankful he didn't feel that in his knees. He held out his hand. The aura wasn't much bigger than a tennis ball. His fingers neared. It seemed to emit a coolness too. Then, as his touch brushed the light, it popped like a blue balloon. He knew the beetle was dead.

Rudolph quickly stood. Starry sunlight shined through the leaves where the lake was waiting Something was happening. The laughing woodpecker was gone. He heard the familiar sound of cars. A dog barked. Of course he recalled what the old man said about the blue glow and the new Death, but it couldn't be true. How could it be?

Did it matter if it made no sense? Rudolph reasoned. The best part of my day is listening to a French lady read a book I can't understand.

The Wall. The Blue Balloon. They didn't matter. For now he would just avoid them.

On either side of the trail, blue glows were scattered like the pearls of a broken necklace. Let them shine, he thought, I'm not going near them. He passed a small blue light caught in a spider's web and hurried on.

CHAPTER SIX:
Fishing

The only option seemed to be back to the bench and the oak tree where Death disappeared. Rudolph sat there and stared at the flat plain of water before him. He knew that behind him, and the brush on either side, would be twinkling with blue. Rubbing his eyes wouldn't make it go away. He also knew the longer he sat on the bench, the more the lights grew. They were there but he was afraid to look. He had eyes for dying—he could see every stricken bird, bug, rabbit, or deer.

Lake Pardon was big enough that you couldn't see it all from any one place. From Rudolph's bench, he could view the tree covered hills on the other side, turning gold with the setting sun. People would be heading home. He didn't think he could. Is this what Death had done all day?

Loud voices caught his attention and Rudolph turned towards the dock on his right. It was framed by maple leaves, its wooden slats stretching twenty feet off shore. Two people sat on chairs at the end and their voices carried in the air. They had been fishing quietly from that spot for hours, but now they were loud as carpenters.

Rudolph could see quite easily what was happening. One of them held a blue glowing fish that wouldn't die. Knives couldn't cut it, the noise of the hammer blows wouldn't stun it. It flicked its tail and swam in the air and fought until its wriggling and sheer power of disbelief got it free. In two blue hops, it was off the dock, into a splash and gone.

It got away but Rudolph had a feeling when the sun went down he would see it again, underwater, along with any other blue things that couldn't die. "You will learn what you need to do," the old man told him. Rudolph had an idea: If I'm the new Death, I have to touch them all. How?

He watched the men on the dock. They were done for the day. What were they going to say? Another one of those impossible fishing stories? Enormous fish that got away. Mermaids, serpents, German submarines. Rudolph watched them hurry, pick up their rods and go. They looked pretty spooked. Maybe they would stay silent about what happened. It had to be seen to be believed.

Almost like some electrical thing, the lake was shutting down for the night. People were going back to cars or riding bicycles home. There was a yellow gate that would be locked and the parking lot would be empty. Then it would only be moonlight, dark trees and the black bowl of water...but not for Rudolph. Around him, like the lights of a city there were little blue glows and the lake was a window to more.

"I'm not doing it," he said, "I'm not being Death." Oh no, he thought, how loud did I say that? It was just the sort of thing a lunatic would yell, alone on a park bench with nighttime falling.

Then another thought came out of the blue.

That beetle was waiting for me...I tried to help it live, but it wanted to die.

That was true.

From the looks of things he was needed all around the lake. The darkness only showed him more. If he accepted the old man's gift to him, he would be walking all night, turning out lights...And what about the glows under the lake? Was he meant to go swimming after them? He pictured himself, holding his breath, plodding along the bleak furrowed floor of Lake Pardon, picking up crawdads and taking down dead fish suspended like ornaments around him. No wonder the old man passed the job along to him. It was only day one and Rudolph was ready to retire.

a part of something bigger

CHAPTER SEVEN:
Wave

It was too late for anyone to be out in the lake. The park was one big shadow, but there was somebody standing up in a canoe, or on a paddleboard, it was hard to tell, but whoever it was, they were getting closer.

Rudolph didn't know what time it was, he didn't wear a watch, it was plenty dark though, and whoever that was coming his way, they were only lit by the moon. Their arms were moving. Their legs were walking. Was it someone walking on water?

Rudolph stood up from the bench. Yes, somebody was walking on the water. He was witnessing another miracle.

Though Rudolph must have been cloaked in shadows, the person knew exactly where he was, as if Rudolph had his own blue glow.

Rudolph waved and the person waved back. At least it wasn't sinister—a park ranger coming to arrest him couldn't walk on top of the lake. It looked like a mechanic, like someone you would see in a car garage changing tires. "Hello," Rudolph said. There wasn't much space between them now.

"Good evening," a man answered him. "Nice night, isn't it?" The sky was full of starlight, the woods and water too, "Why don't you walk on out here?"

"What?" It was bizarre to look at someone standing on something he should be falling through.

The man laughed. "You probably haven't tried it yet, have you? This is your first day, isn't it?" Surprisingly, the man stood on one leg then put it down and gave a hop. He landed without a splash. The lake could have been a marble floor. "You'll be fine. You're like me now."

Rudolph walked down the embankment, onto the sand and with two steps found himself standing on the water too. It was easy. His feet were like the lily pads.

"Welcome to the club," the man said.

"Are you Death too?"

"No. My name is Lenny Wilkens." He touched the nametag sewn to his coat. "You don't have to call yourself Death."

"I'm Rudolph."

"Good to meet you."

"Nobody explained any of this to me. Some old timer on the bench just told me I was the new Death."

Lenny shook his head, "I'm not surprised. That old Death was a real grouch. How much did he tell you?"

"Practically nothing. He said he chose me and I would figure it out."

"Typical," Lenny said.

"I don't know what's going on," Rudolph burst. "I tried to cross the road and I couldn't get home. Am I stuck here? Am I supposed to kill everything before I can go home?"

Lenny smiled. "It seems pretty crazy at first. I remember. I'm like you. I'm Death, you're Death. There are a lot of us. We go all around the planet. We each have our own little territory. I cover the other side of the lake, the forest over there, all the way up the hill and down to the road and the grocery store plaza. You have this lake. It's up to us to make sure the balance is maintained. The balance of life and death is important, Rudolph."

"Of course."

"But, you know, when you look around yourself, you can tell it's got a little out of hand."

"All the blue glows?"

"Right. Those are all lives that have come to the end. For whatever reason—we're not in control of that—we just have to be sure to help them move on."

Rudolph saw a fish appear. It floated slowly like a phosphorescent submarine. It seemed numb and hopeless as that beetle he met. Rudolph rolled up his sleeve. He supposed he would have to bend down and reach in the water for it. "This is going to be a long night if I have to touch every blue glowing thing."

"No, you don't," Lenny said. "All you need to do is wave."

"Wave?"

"Give it a wave goodbye."

Rudolph opened his clenched fingers and made a flat hand. "Goodbye," he told the fish and waved.

So simply, the fish turned from blue to a dark that made it lost in the water.

"That's the way," Lenny said. "Now you just wave to the rest of them."

Rudolph took a look at all the blue lights. He didn't know their stories, they were lights like stars in the night. "What if I don't?" he said.

"You have to," Lenny replied. "That's what you do. That's what I do. I follow the rules. I wear the uniform." He tugged at his zippered coat. "If we don't, everything falls apart."

"I don't like doing this," Rudolph said.

"It's not about you anymore. You're a part of something bigger. And here's the thing, Rudolph—when you help them die, someone else will be helping life come back."

Rudolph could see his smile.

"That's a whole other thing," Lenny grinned. "A separate department, as they say."

Rudolph rubbed his eyes. When he opened them, he took a last look at all the waiting blue souls and—what else could he do?—he started to wave.

CHAPTER EIGHT:
Questions

After Lenny Wilkens left, Rudolph thought of all the questions he should have asked. First of all, was he still alive? He felt alive. But who thinks about whether they're alive or stuck in some dream? Didn't he have a job to do and wasn't he doing it? Wasn't that what every living creature did?

He found that he had walked out near the middle of the lake. The water was like a wet marble floor.

Across the reflection of cloudy night sky were the wooded hills and Lenny was up in there somewhere, walking like Rudolph. They had their territories. That's what Lenny said. The whole world was parceled out to them.

He stood there thinking, listening to the sound of a distant train coming from the bay, on the other side of the wall. Rudolph patted the lake with his shoe. That was another thing he should have asked Lenny about—were they stuck inside their territories? Did the wall keep them in? He took an aimless step onto a cloud. Then Rudolph wondered, How did Lenny leave his territory and walk into mine? Are there doors I can learn to see?

It would be nice if I could go back to the motel. Did he need to though? He wasn't tired. He wasn't hungry. I should be though, shouldn't I?

Then he reminded himself: no, he wasn't the same. Something very strange had happened; he could walk on water, he could end life with his hand.

He heard a jet thousands of feet above him. He caught sight of the tiny dot of it racing along. He supposed there were also bats and owls and moths and other creatures he couldn't see. If they needed him they would be blue.

Rudolph didn't want to go back to that old bench. He felt like sitting somewhere, but not there.

Another question: what happened to Old Death? Did he really melt into a tree? He was sick and worn out from his job, Rudolph remembered, so will that happen to me?

He needed a good place to go and began to walk. It was the opposite of a lonely bench stuck in the briar.

Also, Rudolph could see the beginnings of dawn on the western hills. That side of the lake was the baseball field, picnic tables under shelters, and the playground. Hours from now, Simone would be parking in the lot. He had to see if any of this made sense to her.

A single bird began to chirp.

He didn't want to get caught at sunrise standing in the middle of the lake. He hurried towards the wide clearing. What had he become? He felt like a vampire lurking about. Ghost or not, he wasn't racing for a shadowy crypt—he remembered another place to rest—it was a bench not far from the ballfield, placed perfectly between two willow trees and angled at the lake so you could watch the water and also the park.

As he neared land, there were autumn leaves held to the surface like murky hands. They felt around his shoes.

A gradual shade of purple softened the black outline of the hills. Rudolph stepped onto the beach and climbed the rough embankment. When was the last time he saw a new day begin? A few mornings at 3, when he couldn't sleep—he would make a cup of coffee and sit by the window. That wasn't the same as being out in it. He wondered if he would ever return to the Evergreen.

He should have asked Lenny how long being Death had to last.

The two willow trees and the bench waited for him. His footsteps led out of the lake and pressed in the sand and dirt and went wet and fading onto the path. An early morning detective would find that very curious.

CHAPTER NINE:
The Blind Man

It was hard to tell exactly how it happened. Maybe Rudolph wasn't paying close enough attention. Somehow the lake had gone all foggy. The trees over there on Lenny Wilkens' side were swirled in fog—that was probably where it came from. Like some Japanese fairytale, it poured across the lake and made the bird songs sound like the shroudy notes of an old record player.

Rudolph was on his new bench. He wasn't tired. He was awake to whatever was happening in the new world. The leaves of the willows dragged around him like curtains. Three deer walked past him, skirting the edge of the baseball field. People started to appear. The first ones arrived in their green electric cars. The two men didn't notice Rudolph though he sat on the bench like a spectator as they cleaned and moved on to the next shelter, the little humming wheels crackling on the gravel. Other people began to show: a jogger, a woman with a white dog, someone in a silvery boat that sewed like a needle across the patches of fog. Where was all that fog disappearing? It was hard to keep your attention on, even for Rudolph, with nothing else to do. It foraged in the trees, it hovered on the water and it hung in the air like cold winter breath. It moved as if it could be all one sinuous ghostly torn creature reaching across the lake. And then, the next thing you knew, it was gone.

The dew was the same way, sparkling all over the grass, while the sunshine was sipping it up. The slats of the bench were wet. Rudolph's clothes were damp. He probably looked like a shipwrecked sailor propped beside the lake to dry. Given this much time to watch the world was a gift, a meditation that connected him to the lake with every breath. Things came and went, but at least there was no blue. Not yet.

Rudolph stood. He wasn't tired, hungry, thirsty or sore. He wasn't feeling like a person who spent all afternoon and night at a park. The morning felt no different than the day before.

The lake was attracting more people now: the ones who liked to begin their routine here, and the path behind Rudolph's bench was becoming their road. The thought that had been tumbling about in Rudolph's mind was now polished and smooth as a river stone—what if he was a ghost and couldn't be seen? Is that why Old Death appeared to him—was he already dead? Nobody seemed to notice him, nobody had said a word.

He could hear his feet when his shoes scuffed the ground. They made a dent in the soil. He cleared his throat and said, "Hello," and the sound wasn't dust. Could others see him though? He would have to find out. He buttoned his coat and crossed the worn grass and dipped his feet into the gravelly streambed of the path. 2.6 miles from here all the way around and back; he would let it take him for a spin like a slow fairground ride. He would find out if he wasn't some funhouse ghost, or shadow slipped from a tree. All he wanted to say was good morning and all he wanted to hear was a reply.

Funny, as Rudolph started around he thought of all those years he spent in routine: getting up, going to work, going back home. He could have been on a track. This had to be better than that. He had no idea what the day would bring. First off, he just wanted to make sure he was alive.

Down the path from him, rounding the

blue garbage can on the edge of the ballfield, Rudolph could see someone approaching. A man walking a dog. As they neared, it became clear that it was more a case of the dog leading the man. The man wore thick black glasses and apparently was blind. The dog was carefully watching where they were going. Its brown eyes caught on Rudolph and Rudolph smiled, pleased that his presence had been detected.

Rudolph greeted them, "Hello," when they were only twenty feet away.

The blind man said, "Nice day today."

"Yes it is," Rudolph agreed. But as they passed each other Rudolph thought, "How does he know? He smiled. It was the sort of thing he would point out to Simone if she was here. As he thought about it though it made sense. Of course the blind man could feel the warm sun and the birds were singing. A nice day didn't have to be seen. Rudolph looked forward to telling Simone how he discovered this lesson.

CHAPTER TEN:
Beverley

An hour later Rudolph returned to his spot on the bench. It was already a different day—a blue sky with a few clouds painted on. A duck loudly flapped the water taking off. Rudolph had a good view of the bird as it turned into a dot. The sky was so big the dot got lost in it. What else was hiding out of sight? A circus elephant tied to balloons could be in that cloud. The sky was as wide as the land. Was there even a moon last night? Rudolph couldn't remember seeing it. It seemed like the sort of natural wonder he should have noticed. But his mind was on other things, walking on the water. He noticed more people around and not far behind him the playground sang with little voices. It was almost as if the lake became its own small town. Rudolph rested an arm across the back of the bench and wondered if he was here long enough would they make him the mayor or the town crackpot? Anyway, he liked it. He felt fine, comforted and warm as if the lake was giving him sustenance and keeping him alive.

"Excuse me," someone said, a woman's

voice close to him. "Are you Rudolph?"

I used to be, he thought. When he turned he saw a woman his age and he wondered if he knew her. Her eyes kept her bright, surrounded by lines.

"Simone sent me to look for you," she said. "I'm a friend of hers."

"Oh," he said, "well, you found the right guy. I'm Rudolph." By now he was standing and he tipped his hat.

"I'm Beverley. It's nice to meet you. Simone has told me about you."

"Where is Simone?" On top of everything else he didn't want to find out something happened to her.

"Don't worry, she's fine. She just couldn't make it here today. She sent me to let you know."

"That was nice of her. And you too, thank you." He had to smile. Of course Beverley hadn't brought bad news, she didn't appear that way at all. She was just like a bird coming to his window.

"I'm glad I didn't have to walk too far to tell you," she said. "It's a big lake and my leg gets sore."

"I'm sorry."

"It's alright. It's arthritis. Sometimes it's an old ghost dance partner who won't let go. Other days he stays away. Those days are better."

She laughed and again Rudolph thought she looked familiar. Had they met before? It would have been a long time ago. Maybe he was her dance partner, clumsy and stepping on her toes.

"Will you walk me back to my car?" she asked.

"Sure." He wasn't tired at all. He knew that didn't seem right for his body to have lost certain feelings, but it was like he almost said, he wasn't the Rudolph he used to be.

"Simone told me you two walk around the lake every day."

"Yes, with Sylvie too." Rudolph matched her pace, slower than he went earlier. Maybe Beverley's leg was bothering her again. Sure enough, she took his arm.

"I don't usually walk too much anymore," she said. "I hope you don't mind."

Of course he didn't mind. He liked her hand on top of his arm. It was nice to have someone close by.

A dog ran after a tennis ball on the wide yellowy field.

"No rain this summer," Beverley said and her eyes strayed to the sky.

A bee rushed them making a wild orbit trailing blue and with a flick of his hand Rudolph knocked it from the air. No more roaming flowers for it, filling honeycombs.

"Somewhere far out at sea," said Beverley, "there's condensation. The water molecules are forming precipitation in cumulonimbus and nimbostratus clouds. All it takes is a little wind and the rain is headed our way."

"Ahah!" Rudolph halted. He looked her in the eyes. "That's why I know you! You were the weather reporter on the news for all those years. Beverley Day! You were the only reason to watch TV."

She laughed and he explained, "When I got up in the dark, I would wait until 6:15 to see what you said the weather would be." He could still see her then in front of arrows, letters, numbers, with pictures of rainclouds or sunshine. He laughed with her and shook his head, "I knew you were familiar."

The cars were parked overlooking the lake and he led her up the slope towards their headlight eyes.

"When they let you go, I stopped watching

the news. It doesn't matter as much what happens and the weather can do whatever it wants to."

She squeezed his arm.

Another crow flew over them in the direction of Rudolph's invisible wall.

"That's my car," Beverley said. "Thank you for walking with me. You know it wasn't just for your pleasant company. I have something for you." She stopped at the back of her car and keyed the trunk open. "This leg isn't all bad," she told him. "Actually, it's improved my predictions beyond any weather satellite or chart. It tells me when there's a change in the atmosphere. You're going to be needing this." She reached in and got him an umbrella. It was smooth and pointed as a cormorant.

CHAPTER ELEVEN:
Deserts

Rudolph wasn't alone on his bench for long. A girl appeared with her school backpack and sat at the other end. She dropped the backpack between them, unzipped it and took out a notebook. As she hummed, she turned pages in the binder until she found the page she wanted and put her hand on it. Her song stopped and she spoke, "Do you know about deserts?"

"I know some things about deserts."

"Good," she said. Then she read out loud what was written on the page: "A small airplane crash lands in the desert with 4 people on board." Her eyes darted from the paper to make sure Rudolph was listening.

He was. He could see the little silver plane plowed into the sand, with nothing but dunes around it.

"They are lucky nobody is hurt, but he plane cannot work. The pilot estimates it will take 8 days to walk across the desert." She looked at Rudolph again.

His eyes were closed.

"Are you listening?"

"Yes," he said. "I'm picturing it. They're really in trouble." He opened his eyes. "Do they have water?"

"I'm getting to that," she told him. "They decide to walk to find help. Each person can carry a 5 day supply of water." She glanced at him.

Rudolph's eyes were closed again. He was in the desert with them, holding a can of water in each hand. They were heavy. He had to walk for 8 days dragging these along? Under a hot desert sun and a cold desert moon? The pilot looked like he could make it. He grinned at them like Clark Gable and struck a cigarette. The professor, an Egyptologist, who sat across the aisle from Rudolph and read from a thick book about pyramids looked parched already. The third passenger was a lady dressed in a white sort of safari suit with a wide brimmed hat. She sat in the front row and didn't make a sound as the plane hit the ground. Rudolph thought she may be the most able to survive. Rudolph was the fourth passenger and he knew himself.

The girl's voice continued, "If all 4 of them start out together, how can at least 1 of them make it across the desert and the others return safely to their crashed plane to wait for help?"

Rudolph could hear the desert wind rattle the torn metal wings. They stood at the top of a dune and looked at the hot dry miles ahead of them. The Egyptologist, played by George Zucco, was deep in some dark thought. The Ingrid Berman-like woman tied her hat beneath her chin. The pilot gave a wave to get them started. He was anxious; they could talk on the way.

"Well," the girl said. "What do you think?"

Rudolph opened his eyes and saw that she held a pencil now, hovered over the page of her notebook. "Oh," he said, "there are so many unforeseen things that could happen…8 days walking in a desert…I think the pilot is okay, and the lady, but I don't trust that other man on the plane—the one who's looking for pyramids. You better watch your water with him around. In the morning you might wake to find it all gone, with his footsteps leading off to the nearest mirage."

"It's a story problem," said the girl. "For math class. You're supposed to add and subtract numbers."

"Well, sometimes there is no easy answer."

She sighed.

He insisted, "What if it starts to rain on the second day? What if another plane spots them? There might be a caravan a hundred camels long just over the next dune. We don't know." He saw the look on her face. "I'm sorry. You probably want me to use math."

"Yes," she said. "You have to add up everybody's water and figure out how long it will last." She kicked her legs. Her feet didn't quite touch the ground.

"Well, I thought you wanted to know about deserts," he said, "and if there's one thing I know about deserts, they're unpredictable. So I would say the answer to that story problem is that it's up in the air."

"Up in the air?"

"It's a mystery. Like this umbrella I'm holding. Why do I have an umbrella when the day is so nice? You know why?"

"Why?"

"Because a lady's leg said it was going to rain!"

The girl made a face and they both laughed.

The girl closed her notebook. Then after a moment she opened it again and found the page. "So I'll just write there is no answer?"

Rudolph said, "No. There's an answer. We

just don't know what it will be."

She shrugged and closed her notebook. She was quiet. She paused and said, "Maybe I'll ask someone else."

"That's fine," he smiled. He didn't blame her. She was just looking for a number.

When she was gone it got quiet again and he listened to a raven calling somewhere and the desert and those stranded passengers faded from his thoughts. A little later he felt the first raindrop land on his hand.

CHAPTER TWELVE:
Seeing Blue

It was like a lake had been kept locked away all summer long in some mountain castle room. Now it was released, the rain came down in a fury. All across Pardon in front of Rudolph the surface boiled and the ground around the bench was glazed with an inch of running, bubbling water. At first there were a few screams as people ran off to cars, but now he was all alone with the sound of it.

The rain had taken over the land the way the buffalo used to.

He thought about Beverley. She was right about the rain. She saw this on the way and it was a good thing too—the umbrella she gave him held up a waterfall. He couldn't see the sky above the big black circle opened over him, all the spokes like a bicycle wheel, but it seemed as if a faucet handle had been turned. It poured for a while and then the rain was slowing down. It only beat like one carpenter on the umbrella skin, fewer and fewer and then the soft drops stopped. He was in a symphony that had quieted down and he watched the light come back and heard the birds start to sing.

This would usually be a thankful time to admire the calm startup of the world but not for the new Rudolph. He was seeing blue.

Juncos and chickadees shook the wet leaves. Rudolph stood and collapsed his black umbrella. He didn't use umbrellas but he was glad he had this one—it had left a dry circle on the park bench. The umbrella looked like a cormorant again, folded tight and soaked from hunting in the sea. He left it leaned on the seat and walked towards the shore.

What a lot of water had come down to join the lake. The sloping ground was finger painted with little rivers. Out in the middle of Lake Pardon, a foggy layer of steam burred in the sunlight.

He chose his steps carefully. The slick dirt was slippery, he didn't want to fall and slide like a wheelbarrow into the reeds.

Not everyone comes through a storm okay. The casualties waited for him.

Wouldn't most people think twice before leaving land? Not Rudolph. Not anymore. He was so sure of his new life he didn't break stride as he wandered out ghostly onto the water. The soles of his shoes dripped like paddlewheels.

About five feet out, he turned and parted the cattails that grew like curtains. Minnows scattered from the cloudy shape of him above.

He pushed his way through the snapping reeds and stepped on lily pads. Something very blue was waiting for him.

It was a duck. Rudolph guessed it must have fallen in the storm. Getting close to it wasn't easy. It was wedged in with broken branches and tangled in fishing line. Rudolph wanted to pick it up and soothe it and try to heal it but he would find he wasn't that person anymore. The moment he touched the soft feathers, the blue went out of it and the bird was dead.

The lake would be reviving soon. People would be reappearing, and Rudolph backed out of the overgrown shoreline trying not to cause attention. He hurried across the top of the water back onto the sand, looking more like a heron than a man. He glanced at the park as he climbed the slope, the rocks and roots and tufts of grass, and was glad nobody stood nearby on the lawn staring at him. Luck had been with him. Death had snaked out over the water, struck and snuck back to the green painted bench.

Rudolph took a deep breath and sighed.

He sat on the dry circle next to his umbrella and he clapped his hands. Every blue light he could see winked from view.

The lake was quiet. All around the edges and up the hillside over there, the leaves were turning colors. Why weren't they blue? Wasn't that the color of dying? Apparently not for trees—their leaves burned like fire, yellow and red, before they fell to the ground.

Rudolph turned to face the playground the baseball field, the shelter, and in case his clap didn't carry back there, he clapped his hands again. He was surprised he could still be startled by something strange. His hands didn't make any sound. There wasn't a sound anywhere. It was as if he went deaf.

When he said, "Hey!" there was nothing—his voice had been plucked from the air. He felt like shouting in a photograph. There was hollow silence and the park was frozen, untouched by wind or the motion of any living thing.

Rudolph turned to look at the lake again. The water was stretched flat, slightly wrinkled like a bedspread, but it was just more of the same still photograph. Some ducks were anchored off shore. Sun shined with a steady light, clouds were hung in place, not a shadow wavered.

He was afraid he was put in another new world where he was the only one undead. Everything was stuck. He could move across it like a moth on a painting. This seemed to be his fate. He seemed to be marooned even more than before. Time had stopped and he was the only one aware. Now what was he meant to do, having gone past death and time? There was nothing to listen to, nothing to watch, only the lake frozen as the moon before him. What he wouldn't give for a bird or a leaf falling to the ground. When he looked at his hands he wondered if they had turned blue and if this was what it felt like, waiting for your end.

CHAPTER THIRTEEN:
The Meeting

It was the smallest motion on the other side of the lake. Like a tiny spider crawling the rim of a brick, it moved on that thin dark line between water and land. Then, as Rudolph watched, it split and became two specks of movement walking on the lake. Two people, he guessed. Rudolph had a pretty good idea who one of them was, but if it was Lenny Wilkens who was he bringing with him? They neared and Rudolph was quite sure one of them was Lenny. He recognized the uniform they both wore.

Rudolph stood and went back to the shore and his shoes were noiseless on the glassy lake. The water didn't even stick to his soles. He saw Lenny raise his arm and Rudolph returned the wave. They were getting close, but Rudolph wondered what they would say. He remembered the deaf custodian at the office where he used to work. Rudolph learned a little bit of sign language from him. All he could recall was hello and goodbye.

Lenny and his companion, a woman,

walked briskly and Rudolph swore he could hear the faint brush of their feet on the surface. If it was wishful thinking it seemed to be true. He was sure he could hear their slushy approach. Yes, they even left a ripple in their wake.

"Hello Rudolph," Lenny called.

The words came at him like a splash. Rudolph tried to reply, but he was still barely more than a ghost afloat above the water.

"He's not awake yet," said the woman next to Lenny.

"Oh yeah."

Rudolph heard the zipper on Lenny's coat as he reached into a pocket and took out something small enough to fit inside his hand.

Rudolph waited on his quiet space for them to get to him. The lake crumpled like newspaper under them. He could read the names sewn on their jackets: Lenny and Maria.

"Hello again," Lenny smiled. "You're probably feeling a little lost." He held out his hand. "Here, this will help."

What Rudolph felt put into his hand was a smooth stone. He stared at it.

"Go ahead," Lenny said, "hold it tight."

As soon as his fingers tightened into a fist

around the rock, Rudolph almost dropped it. He suddenly heard the sound of his own wild breathing and felt the tremors from a booming, beating heart. He exhaled loud as a whale and asked, "Can I talk again?" answering himself with the next breath, "Yes, I can."

Maria laughed. "Lenny was supposed to give you that stone before."

"Sorry," Lenny said, "I forgot."

Rudolph patted the lake with his shoes. He whistled a little and made a song of it.

"This is Maria," Lenny said, finally introducing her. "She's from the next district after mine."

"Hi," he said, lowering his voice—was he shouting?—"I'm Rudolph."

She shook his hand and Rudolph said, "Nice to meet you. Are you at the grocery store?"

She said, "Yes, and the plaza and the road."

Rudolph guessed, "There's probably not much death around there."

She looked around at the quiet postcard lake and said, "That's what I was thinking about here."

Rudolph laughed and nodded.

"Dying is everywhere," Lenny said and for

a second Rudolph wondered what they must look like—these figures standing on a lake talking about death. But the rest of the world was still frozen, nobody could see them.

Rudolph cleared his throat and asked, "So what exactly is going on? What happened to everything?"

"Everything has sort of gone to sleep for a while," Lenny said, "except for us."

"We have a meeting to go to," Maria explained. "All the Deaths do. And we're running a little late."

"That's true," Lenny said. "We should get going."

"Oh," said Rudolph as he turned and joined them heading back to his shoreline. "Where's the meeting?"

"Not far."

The three of them splashed quickly across the lake.

"How long do I need to hold this rock?" Rudolph asked them. It was clenched tight in his fist.

"That will get you to the meeting and back here again," Maria said. She opened her hand to show him the stone she carried. "When you return, you won't need it anymore." She pretended to throw it at the lake. "There's a lot of old stones like this lying around."

"Right," said Rudolph, "I bet."

They made land and Lenny led them onto the path Rudolph knew so well. When Lenny and Maria stopped before a wall of blackberry and Lenny said, "We're here," Rudolph grinned at the joke. Were the other Deaths here in front of him pinned to the vine in the form of withered hard berries that were never picked? Would they all chime out for the meeting to start?

CHAPTER FOURTEEN:
Lynn

The door of blackberry opened and Rudolph hurried through. When it shut behind him it was lost in the thorns and blackened leaves.

Rudolph laughed. He couldn't believe what he had just done. All those years in meetings, all the time he wasted at the office in a closed room sitting around a table looking at charts, listening to words that were dull and repetitious as a monotony machine. When Lenny and Maria took him into a room like that again, filled with Deaths in uniform and lines and letters drawn on a chalkboard, Rudolph told them he would be right back. What an escape! He felt like Houdini staring at that blackberry wall with its hidden seams. Before anything could go wrong, Rudolph raised his arm and threw the stone at the lake.

That tiny almost unheard plop made everything come to life again. It happened so suddenly Rudolph swayed and nearly fell on the path. Can you imagine nearly nothing and then the world becomes a carrousel?

The spell was broken.

A bicycle went by him.

A crow cawed from a tree.

A yellow leaf spiraled towards the ground.

He could hear a dog barking from further along the shore and a hundred other sounds and smells far and near. He wished he had that umbrella so he could lean on it. It would take him a minute to get used to the world.

"Rudolph!"

Funny, with all the sound around him, all it took was one word to know who it was. Lynn's voice was a bird apart from all the others.

"Are you alright, Rudolph?"

"I just need to catch my breath," he slowly said.

"Let's find somewhere to sit down." Her hair, tied back, turned with her words. She took his arm and started for the nearest shelter by the playground, but Rudolph pointed at the water.

"I have a bench over there."

She had been running around the lake. While everything was frozen, she must have been caught in stride. Strange, Rudolph thought, that he didn't see any people during that time. They must have been there though…

she must have been nearby all the while to find him so soon after the world restarted. He tried not to step on a dandelion and her grip on him tightened.

"Careful."

"It's okay," he told her. "I was a little dizzy but I'm alright now."

The bench was in the sun. It looked dry. The umbrella was awkward with no raindrops in sight. When they sat down, she moved the umbrella aside. She turned to face him. Her bare knees pressed together.

He noticed the college name on the t-shirt she wore. "How's school going?" he asked her. Then before she could answer, he remembered, "You know, before the rain today I was helping another girl with her homework. She was sitting right there."

Lynn shook her head and gave him an owlish look instead of something to say.

"I'm sorry," he said, "I've been doing a lot of walking lately. Maybe I'm getting tired."

"Well you do look better now, but you sure gave me a scare."

He said, "I appreciate the concern. It's nice to have a friend like you."

"And you didn't stop by the desk yesterday.

You usually do, to get your room key."

"I know."

"Will you tonight?"

"I hope so. I'll try."

"Hmmmm," she said and her eyes said something again then she looked at her feet. The gravel path turned to dirt in the woods and had colored the bright sides of her shoes.

He told her, "I've been spending more time at the lake. I sort of hate to see summer go, I guess I need to enjoy it here as long as I can before the weather gets worse."

"Well, you've got your umbrella."

"Right." But he wondered what he would do in a month or two when it got cold enough to snow. Last winter the lake iced over. He might not be the only one walking on it. "Are you on the way to the motel?"

She nodded. "Do you want me to bring you anything?"

He chuckled. It was odd she would say that. She didn't know he was trapped here, did she? It was possible she could have checked his room. She would have worried where he was. She might have looked again today and seen he still wasn't there. She would have gone for her run, thinking about him, and then there he was by the blackberries, crumpled and staggered like someone homeless. It didn't look good, but she would like the truth even less.

She stood up and told him she better go. Their goodbyes weren't the usual ones. Rudolph held back telling her how he was part of the lake. He was cursed. How could it help for her to know?

There were more clouds in the sky. He stared at their reflections as they moved slowly over the water to become shadows on the forested hill.

He could tell Simone though…She wouldn't just stare with the wide blue eyes of a fairytale. She had seen the world. But where was she? Beverley didn't say. She was nowhere in sight and a day without her to talk to could be felt.

CHAPTER FIFTEEN:
Minus One

He didn't have a lot but he had time. While the day worked its way towards sundown Rudolph sat on the bench and waved his hand every once in a while. Little creatures twinkled out of existence. That wasn't bad; it was like brushing off sand. He didn't have to know what they were to see them gone.

Not quite an hour after Lynn left, while he was still thinking about how much she knew and if he should tell someone he was no longer the same, he saw a big ball of blue on the lake. Someone clung to their overturned kayak. Rudolph knew how simple it was to make it stop. His job wasn't hard, a child could do it. As he ran along the edge of lake he supposed there were children somewhere being Death. All it took was the strict observance of following the rules. Rudolph broke them when he got to the man sitting in the lawn chair, eyes closed to the sun, a trailer full of rental boats minus one. Death shouldn't have woken that man and sent him out paddling to save someone who was meant to drown.

Rudolph sat on his bench and watched the last bit of orange sun go down. The trees outlined on the hill glowed like jagged teeth as the night began.

He had a lot of time to think.

He saw the bats flicker back and forth. A few stars were already out. The lake was calm. On the water Lenny Wilkens was walking his way.

"Oh no," Rudolph groaned. He stood up. He left his umbrella on the bench and headed toward the path. The gravel was gray like a streambed and he walked quickly, along the moon colored baseball field, past the chain link backdrop scooped big enough to catch a bus. Some night bird swooped over the big expanse. Rudolph couldn't remember what the bird was called—when Lynn brought him his book he could look it up. There was a deer watching him from the parking lot. Rudolph knew he wouldn't outrun Lenny Wilkens. Somewhere, probably where the path turned by the bog into woods, he would hear his name called. Rudolph didn't know what he would say. If he was lucky maybe Lenny would just go away. Reaching the shadows of the big fir trees, he thought, if I'm really lucky I'll wake up in my room at the Evergreen and this whole thing will only be a dream.

He could imagine telling Simone all about it. What a story—the Old Death, the blue glows, the invisible wall, the feeling of walking on water.

"Rudolph!"

What's the speed of sound? How fast and how far would he have to run to be beyond the sound of his own name? Rudolph pictured that girl on the bench with her notebook and pencil trying to solve that problem: Another crashed airplane, another vast desert, and people whose lives could be counted in water.

"Rudolph!" It was closer. Lenny must have made shore.

With a sigh, Rudolph stopped walking. The bog beside the path still smelled of skunk cabbage. What little light there was glossed among the lilies and broken branches. For a moment Rudolph thought of running—it had been years since he ran and he felt he could do it—running in the trees like a child again, but he knew Lenny Wilkens would be right after him and Lenny was probably faster. He was thinking about frogs, what a nice home this spot would be for them, when he heard the gravel chirp and scatter on the path behind him. Lenny had been running and now he slowed down.

"Rudolph."

Rudolph turned to face him. Lenny Wilkens had the whole lake poured at his back, dotted with starlight and a moon chipped out of ice.

"I couldn't tell if you could hear me," Lenny said. "I lost track of you at the meeting and it looked like I was losing you again."

"That meeting reminded me of my old job. I spent 25 years going in and out of rooms like that."

"You don't seem to be too enthused about this job," Lenny said.

"No. I'm not. I want to be done doing jobs. I spent my whole life doing them, I'm done with them."

"But this isn't like those old jobs. Now you're practically immortal."

"I don't care. This isn't living. What am I doing going round and round? Why am I killing things? I don't want to take lives to have this life." Rudolph had to catch his breath. His words had been almost reckless and he took a moment to try again in a simpler way. "Anyway, I don't mind being an ordinary person."

They started walking again. The path went past the bog over the brook. Their shoes flicked through the maple leaves, onto the hard packed loam of fir needles, into the nighttime shade of the trees.

It was pretty clear how Rudolph felt about the past few days. Lenny Wilkens listened to him and they even stopped at that bench where Rudolph like to rest in the forest and look across at the other side of the lake. It didn't matter what Lenny said to him, all Rudolph wanted to know was, "How can I go back?"

CHAPTER SIXTEEN:
The Mermaid

Walking on water was one of the real pleasures of Rudolph's occupation. He liked the sound his shoes made. He liked the solitary calm of being out in the middle of the lake with the night sky reflection. He would miss this if anything were to change.

Lenny Wilkens didn't seem to think it could—he said there were ways it could be done, but anyone with a conscience wouldn't like them. He said if Rudolph could lure someone to his bench he could pass the job along to them. That's what the Old Death had done to Rudolph and it was cruel. What a spiderlike thing to do. Rudolph thought of the only ones who had visited him: the girl with her homework, Beverley and Lynn. No, it couldn't be done. It was like Lenny Wilkens told him, Rudolph would just have to get used to being Death. It just took time, Lenny said.

Rudolph stopped and turned around to look at the big black hillside Lenny disappeared back into. A few blue lights were scattered about. The other thing Lenny said was you can't change fates. It wasn't up to them to let a bird live, or save someone on the water who had fallen in. Like some chalkboard slogan Lenny Wilkens told him, "If something is blue you have to follow through." Rudolph flicked his hand at the forest and obeyed. The little stars were gone. It wasn't any better, it wasn't true it didn't hurt if you didn't see them up close or know the story behind the blue.

"Rudolph!" came the shout of his name and water splashing.

His ears told him it was Lynn and he turned, expecting to see her in one of those rental boats with the paddle dug in. There was no boat, the black water crumpled around her bobbing head and her hands thrashed like white flowers around her. Her head went under again as Rudolph ran across the lake to her. She wasn't that far from land but far enough to drown. He had to reach her before the blue.

He slid on his knees and leaned into the lake and caught her under the arms and pulled her up. Her skin was slippery as a seal. She coughed and he held her tighter as she brushed the slick hair from her face. Her body quivered like a fish but he wasn't going to let her sink. "Rudolph."

Right through her skin, he could feel the motion of her legs, her feet paddling to stay close to him. When his eyes left her eyes, he saw all of her was moon colored, skin fading to purple further underwater. He didn't want to drop her but he was so surprised. His eyes went quickly back to her eyes.

"Are you alright, Lynn?" She must have also been stunned, to see him out walking on the water.

He watched her eyes get calm and as she was feeling strong again he started to let her go, but she grabbed his hand. She could have pulled him down in, if water was something he could fall in.

"Hah!" she laughed, "I knew there was something..." she took another deep breath, "different about you." Her grip on his hand was tight.

"What about you?" he said. "What are you doing out in the lake like this?" Maybe she wasn't exactly a person either? He remembered stories about mermaids. They could live on land a while but had to return to water.

Lynn hung from his hand and laughed. "Sometimes I go for a swim after work. It's called skinny dipping, Rudolph. You might have heard of it?"

"Yes, of course." He was surprised he could hold her weight so easily. Death was strong, he never seemed to tire.

She let go of his hand and set her hands on his shoes. "How are you standing though?" she could only feel water around and below him.

Lenny Wilkens never told Rudolph how he was supposed to answer that if he got caught. Being Death wasn't invisible, though it made you a kind of outcast. You became someone who sat on benches and never slept, and walked the rounds like a nightwatchman. "Oh," he sighed, "it's just something I learned to do."

She laughed. "Well it's amazing!"

Her voice seemed to ring across the lake and it made Rudolph nervous. Nobody told him all the rules. Was it safe for Lynn to know? Or at any moment would Lenny Wilkens and Maria come riding across the water like Valkyries?

"It is and it isn't," Rudolph said. "But maybe we should get back to land." The other side of the lake was still dark and haunted, the way he wanted it to be. They weren't far from the shore. He could see the white towel Lynn hung from the branch of a tree.

CHAPTER SEVENTEEN:
A Bird Book

Rudolph left Lynn before she got to land to get dressed and he waited for her at the bench. He watched the water and the black sleeping hills across the lake. He tried to decide how much more to tell her. Should he say to someone that he was Death? And there were others like him watching life and waiting for its time to end?

Everyone, even Lynn, would one day turn blue and he couldn't blame her if she never wanted to see him again…No, he didn't want to tell her that much. She had seen him walking on water, hopefully that was enough. He already told her it was just some strange new affliction that made him anchored to this place. The lake was a magnet. He couldn't leave it. He didn't know why, he said. That was only sort of a lie.

He was happy to finally hear her footsteps. They were quick and light on the gravel, then soft on the grass leading to him.

"Is this where you spend the night now?" she asked. She took a seat next to him.

He nodded. "This is my new motel."

"It's nice, but brrr!" she shivered and rubbed her arms. They were covered again in flannel and a coat. "It's getting cold. That might be my last swim."

"The leaves are falling. Winter won't be long."

She stared at the water too. "I brought your book." She took it from her carry bag. "It was right where you said it would be. Do you need anything else?"

"No." He took the bird book from her. "Thanks. This is all I need now."

"No warmer clothes or a blanket?"

She already asked him that as she slid along in the water next to him, when he told her there was something about his new power to walk on water that didn't let him leave the park. "It's like I told you, I don't get cold anymore. And I don't need to eat anymore, or sleep."

"Then what do you do?"

"I don't know," he lied. "I just am."

She was quiet, thinking. She rubbed her legs and he remembered she was probably cold. Would she want his ragged coat? "Maybe you're here so you can walk on water and save people?" she said.

He smiled. That was funny. It was just the opposite. But he remembered the kayak and pulling Lynn from the water so easily. She was right—there were two people he had saved. He looked at her and she was smiling too. She believed his story, all he had told her, and she believed in him.

Then she blinked and shook her damp hair. "I never expected all this to be happening." She touched his hand for a second then she stood up and crossed her arms. "I better go, Rudolph. I'm freezing!" She grabbed her bag. "I'll see you tomorrow?"

He raised his hands to her and held them flat as if holding a tray with a hot coffee pot. "I'll be here."

"Okay." Lynn took a few steps like she was ready to run, then she turned back to him. "What about your room? It's paid through the month, but what happens after that?"

He laughed. That was the last thing he was thinking about. She was young enough to believe a fairytale but she was practical too. "Oh, Lynn," he said. "Don't worry about that."

What did those few things in a room matter now? He had all he needed. There was even a bird book in his hands. Letting it open, it was too dim to read. Later on he could walk to the shelter and sit under the green light. The moths would keep him company. When was the last time someone read to them? No wonder they crowded around lanterns and light bulbs and bedside lamps—they were waiting to hear about Huckleberry Finn, Myrna Minkoff and Atticus Finch.

The lake was quiet again. Nothing seemed to be happening.

Rudolph thumbed through the dark pages, saw a sparrow on a black tree branch and it occurred to him that most of these birds would eat moths, given a chance. The life of a moth could end at any moment when a swallow or a bluebird was around.

CHAPTER EIGHTEEN:
Willard

Two nights without sleep, without being tired, and his mind must have gone looking for something like dreams. The place the mind projects when the body rests is just as necessary as the one we walk through all day. So it might have been somewhere around 2 or 3 o'clock when he saw a disturbance on the calm surface of the lake.

Less than a hundred feet from him, something moved through the water like a glowing tugboat. There was a blueness to it but not the bright blue he was used to. Rudolph watched it move in a straight line along the shore, no faster than a duck paddling. Apparently it must have just surfaced, how else could Rudolph, the lake watcher, have missed it? It took its time. It was in no hurry. It knew where Rudolph was and it steered that way like a slow bicycle.

Phosphorous. That's the word that popped into Rudolph's head. Sometimes the sea would wash up like that and you could roll up your cuffs and wade in that glow. Someone approached that way, wading waist deep in water, lit by a pale distant streetcar light. But it was deep out there—how long would their legs have to be? Underwater, walking slow as stilts, feet picking over stones and digging toes in the silt.

Rudolph moved uncomfortably on the bench. He decided this was a dream happening and he would find out where it went next.

The wading, barely blue person was a young man. As he reached the shore in front of Rudolph's bench, he walked from the water on ordinary legs, pants that matched the suit coat he wore.

I'm seeing things, Rudolph decided. This is only in my imagination.

The ghostly person didn't leave a ripple on the lake or a mark on sand. No wonder—his feet didn't quite touch the ground—they were wooden as a marionette's stringed shoes. That was strange, but even weirder was the sound coming towards Rudolph. The lake was so silent it was like hearing a flock of geese appearing in the air way up over the trees. They were words. Rudolph couldn't look at the face, the painted eyes staring at him, even when the ghost was standing next to him.

"You can't make it," said the words. "You

can't do anything right. It will never get better." The words mumbled like a cold ticking alarm clock. "There's no point. Give up."

"Who are you?" Rudolph said. Now he saw a surprised boy, the age of Lynn and the chanting words stopped.

"You can see me?"

"Who are you?" Rudolph repeated.

"Oh no…" With a sad puff of a sigh, the ghost—that's what Rudolph figured he was—sat on the other end of the bench. "No one is supposed to see me."

"You're a ghost?"

"I guess so…" His body slumped and he was hazy as a bucketful of phosphorous.

"And you sneak up on people and say those terrible, hopeless things to them?"

"You looked like someone who didn't want to be around anymore."

"That's what you tell people who feel that way?"

"It isn't that bad. I'm just saying what they tell themselves all the time. I'm trying to help them. Not as easy as it sounds…" He reached in his suit pocket. "They don't always listen to me."

Now Rudolph noticed the company logo

on the suit, a harp inside a cloud, with the name Willard stitched below. It wasn't the ghost suit he was buried in, it was a uniform. Willard felt in his coat and found a sort of passport. "I've got seven." He showed Rudolph the stamped page. There were seven different names and red stamps. "Once I get to ten, I get a prize." He returned the little book to his pocket. "Sometimes it takes a while."

Rudolph shook his head, "You work for Death too. We must be all around this lake."

Willard shrugged. "I don't know." He stood again. "I should get going. Sorry I didn't know who you were."

"Don't worry."

Willard shrugged and his feet paddled at the ground like a bicycle rider, down the slope to the water. He quickly sank to his waist and kept moving like one of those pedal boats you can rent. Rudolph watched him until he was no bigger than a duck. Rudolph couldn't tell if he sank or just suddenly disappeared.

deep in a faraway place

CHAPTER NINETEEN:
Walking with a Wish

Daylight arrived without rain. The sky was a clear blue and it was warm enough that morning to see people in their summer clothes again. "I won't get used to this," Rudolph thought. He had been around the lake and seen everyone. "They come here, enjoy their time here, then go on to the rest of their day. I'll be here forever." His bench was waiting just ahead. The only way off it was to switch with someone else who happened along. That still seemed wrong. But he wondered if he could have tricked Willard. Willard was just a kid and he was already dead. This had to be a better job than the one he had. Rudolph sighed. There had to be a way.

As he sat down he noticed something blue. This job was never ending.

The faintest breeze made ripples on the lake. He wondered what would happen if he went out there right now. What if all these people saw him walking on the water? The little boats would circle around him, crowds would gather on the beach, and pretty soon people would hurry to the lake from all over to see him. He would walk back and forth from one side to the other. There would be television cameras and a helicopter would riffle the water. What if he stopped at the nearest microphone held out to him and told everyone what was really going on?

Rudolph smiled. That thought made him laugh. He was sure Lenny Wilkens would freeze time long before that happened. Someone somewhere was probably keeping an eye on him.

"Rudolph." Finally the voice he was waiting for. The sound of the baby stroller too, rattly plastic wheels on the path.

He turned from the lake and said, "Hi Simone!" How long was she gone? "Where have you been? Gee, it's good to see you."

She laughed.

What was wrong with him? He almost felt like crying. He stood up and rubbed the back of his hand across his eyes. The last time he saw Simone, he was still a normal man. How nice to see her smile. She made him feel that way too.

"Is this your new lakeside property?" she asked in nearly a whisper.

He could see Sylvie was already asleep. She

was covered in her French flag blanket. He picked up the umbrella and gave them room on the bench with him. "I like your flowers," he said as she settled.

She held three dandelions that she placed on Sylvie's lap. "She is always looking for flowers. She is like a little bee." Simone straightened the cloth canopy so the sun wasn't on her daughter's face. She was sleeping deep in a faraway place.

"I've been missing your company," Rudolph said. He didn't know what he was going to tell her next. He took a moment to draw a breath, where everything he had seen flickered and spun. The movie lasted only an instant before she spoke.

"Look!" she said and pointed. A leaf was falling from one of the tall trees nearby. It tumbled in the air like a pilot without a parachute. She put her hand on his sleeve and said, "Make a wish."

That wasn't hard for Rudolph; he had been walking with a wish for three days.

There was no way of telling where a leaf was going. Rudolph had seen children on the wooded path running back and forth trying to catch them. After soaring out over the lake where it seemed it would ditch like a plane in the sea, it veered back towards land. There wasn't much air left. Maybe only a leaf knows where it will land.

Simone squeezed Rudolph's arm. The leaf could have been caught in a pigeon's landing pattern as it came down on the bare ground in front of the bench. All it needed was blue feathers and a bobbing head.

Simone clapped her hands quietly. "Bravo! A leaf's last performance," she smiled and glanced at Rudolph, "until the encore." She raised her arm and the thin gold bracelet slid back into her sleeve. With two fingers directed at the ground, she touched the air.

The leaf, crisp, brown and brick colored, suddenly became lime green.

THE LAKE WALKER
Written by Allen Frost
9/11/17—12/1/17

Books by Good Deed Rain

Saint Lemonade, Allen Frost, 2014. Two novels illustrated by the author in the manner of the old Big Little Books.

Playground, Allen Frost, 2014. Poems collected from seven years of chapbooks.

Roosevelt, Allen Frost, 2015. A Pacific Northwest novel set in July, 1942, when a boy and a girl search for a missing elephant. Illustrated throughout by Fred Sodt.

5 Novels, Allen Frost, 2015. Novels written over five years, featuring circus giants, clockwork animals, detectives and time travelers.

The Sylvan Moore Show, Allen Frost, 2015. A short story omnibus of 193 stories written over 30 years.

Town in a Cloud, Allen Frost, 2015. A three-part book of poetry, written during the Bellingham rainy seasons of fall, winter, and spring.

A Flutter of Birds Passing Through Heaven: A Tribute to Robert Sund. 2016. Edited by Allen Frost and Paul Piper. The story of a legendary Ish River poet & artist.

At the Edge of America, Allen Frost, 2016. Two novels in one book blend time travel in a mythical poetic America.

Lake Erie Submarine, Allen Frost, 2016. A two week vacation in Ohio inspired these poems, illustrated by the author.

and Light, Paul Piper, 2016. Poetry written over three years. Illustrated with watercolors by Penny Piper.

The Book of Ticks, Allen Frost, 2017. A giant collection of 8 mysterious adventures featuring Phil Ticks. Illustrated throughout by Aaron Gunderson.

I Can Only Imagine, Allen Frost, 2017. Five adventures of love and heartbreak dreamed in an imaginary world. Cover & color illustrations by Annabelle Barrett.

The Orphanage of Abandoned Teenagers, Allen Frost, 2017. A fictional guide for teens and their parents. Illustrated by the author.

In the Valley of Mystic Light: An Oral History of the Skagit Valley Arts Scene, 2017. Edited by Claire Swedberg & Rita Hupy.

Different Planet, Allen Frost, 2017. Four science fiction adventures: reincarnation, robots, talking animals, outer space and clones. Cover & illustrations by Laura Vasyutynska.

Go with the Flow: A Tribute to Clyde Sanborn. 2018. Edited by Allen Frost. The life and art of a timeless river poet.

Homeless Sutra, Allen Frost, 2018. Four stories: Sylvan Moore, a flying monk, a water salesman, and a guardian rabbit.

The Lake Walker, Allen Frost 2018. A little novel set in black and white like one of those old European movies about death and life.

Coming soon:

A Hundred Dreams Ago, Allen Frost, 2018. A winter book of poetry and prose. Cover and illustrations by Aaron Gunderson.

www.ingramcontent.com/pod-product-compliance
Lightning Source LLC
LaVergne TN
LVHW041646060526
838200LV00040B/1742